WE PLAY

by Phyllis Hoffman • pictures by Sarah Wilson

A CHARLOTTE ZOLOTOW BOOK
HARPER & ROW, PUBLISHERS

WE PLAY

Library of Congress Cataloging-in-Publication Data
Hoffman, Phyllis.
    We play / by Phyllis Hoffman ; pictures by Sarah Wilson.
        p.   cm.
    "A Charlotte Zolotow book."
    Summary: A rhymed account of a child's fun-filled day at nursery
school.
    ISBN 0-06-022557-2 : $. — ISBN 0-06-022558-0 (lib. bdg.) :
$
    [1. Stories in rhyme.   2. Nursery schools—Fiction.   3. Schools—
Fiction.]   I. Wilson, Sarah, ill.   II. Title.
PZ8.3.H673We 1990   89-36381
[E]—dc20   CIP
                                                                  AC

This one's all for Mom—
with love and admiration
for my mother, Bertha Hoffman.
P.M.H.

For Dana
S.W.

We come.

We stay.

We hug.

We play.

We climb.

We slide.

We run.

We hide.

We dance.

We jump.

We whirl.

We bump.

We poke.

We punch.

We cook.

We munch.

We wash.

We sweep.

We read.

We sleep.

We look.

We show.

We wave.

We go.

JP   Hoffman, Phyllis
HOF   We play

DATE DUE			

GAYLORD M2